Transformations

Stories of Sudden
and Astonishing Changes

by

Stanley Longman

Illustrations by
Corah Longman *(cl)*
and Stanley Longman *(sl)*

Bilbo Books Publishing
www.BilboBooks.com
bilbobookspublishing@gmail.com
(706)-549-1597

ISBN- 978-1-7364598-3-6
Printed in the United States of America
All rights reserved. Published in the United States of America by
Bilbo Books Publishing. Athens, Georgia

"Percival's Many Personalities" adapted/inspired by Marcel Ayme's, The Man Who Walked Through Walls, Pushkin Press, 2018.

Table of Contents

List of Illustrations

Introduction

These fourteen tales depict a variety of transformations. Some come about to provide satisfaction for an individual's frustration or longing. That is the case in the story "Sylvie's Flight" in which she is transformed into a butterfly. On a grander scale it is true of Percival, who assumes many personalities through his newfound power that lets him walk through walls. A couple derives pleasure from swimming in a wheat field transformed into a golden sea. Other stories depict an experience much less pleasant, as Rupert Alan Pomeroy discovers when he satisfies his curiosity only to have the Empress condemn him to die. People turn transparent, allowing others to see right through them. There are two stories in which the world depicted in a painting comes to life and either invades our world or folds someone up into its world. In another story, a whole town witnesses fellow citizens disappear mysteriously, one by one.

Every story hinges on a sudden and startling transformation. In each case, the source of the transforming power is simply a given. There is a progression to the stories: the first three stories portray children and the last two death and the Afterlife.

Apologies go to Ovid and Kafka.

A note on the illustrations: the drawings that accompany the stories were created by the author and Corah Longman, his granddaughter.

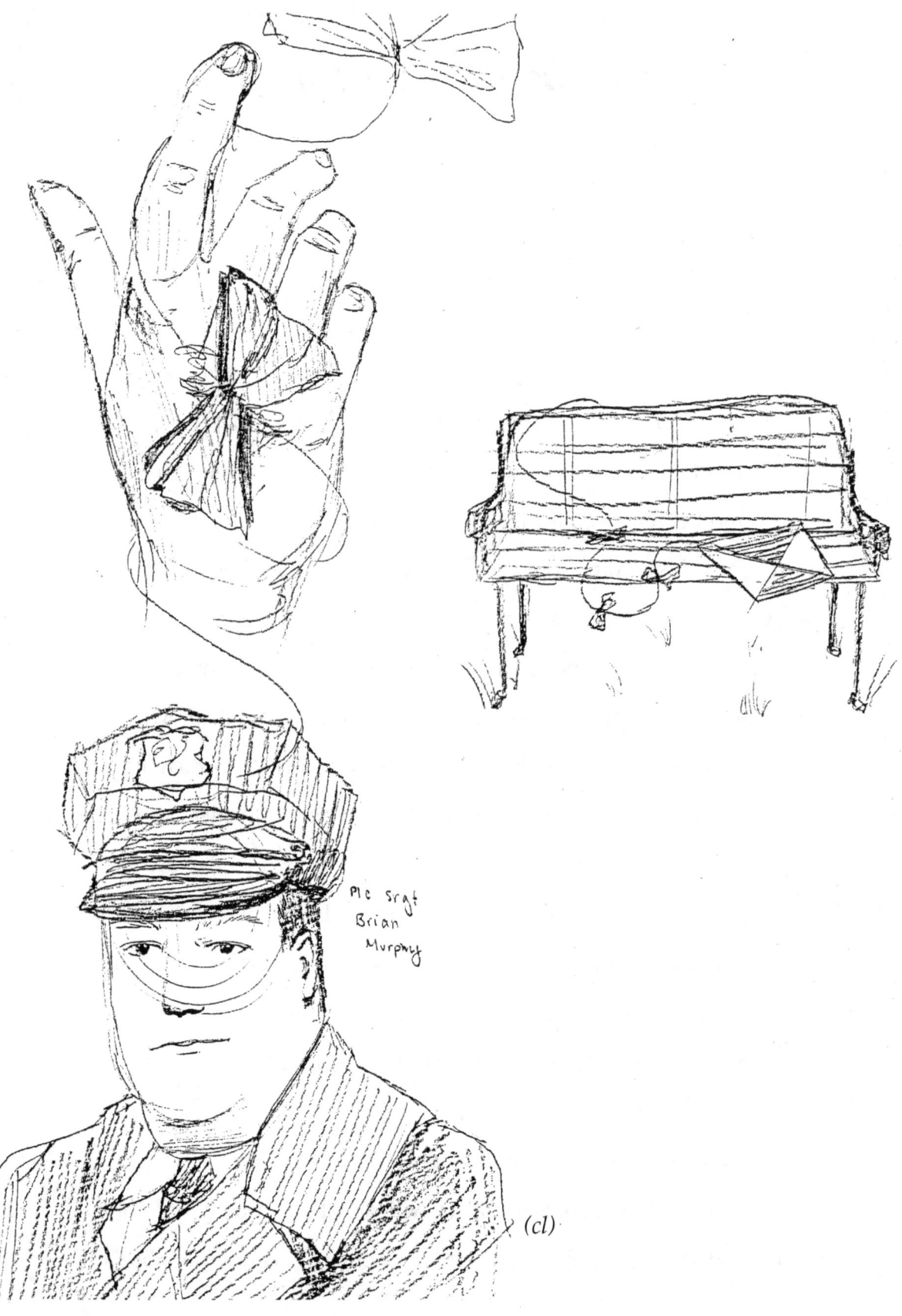

Pfc Srgt
Brian
Murphy

(cl)

A Remarkable Kite

There was a tradition observed every spring in the village of Upper Chester: as soon as the breezes of March kicked in, people knew it was time to start thinking about their kites. Many of them, young and old, took great pride in designing and building their kites. They did produce some colorful and intricate designs and shapes balanced by elaborate tails. This tradition had its time and its place. There was an open field near the edge of town where everybody would gather. Over time it became an organized competition. A particular date was selected for the gathering, usually the second Saturday in April. The competition was strictly controlled, with rules governing how each kite was to be built, how long its tail and how long the string could be. A start time would be issued for each participant and the time each kite stayed aloft was recorded. There were even rules about how the contestants were to conduct themselves.

Police Sergeant Brian Murphy was assigned to watch over the event. He had been doing this duty for a dozen years. He was there again this year. At first it had been entertaining, but he grew weary of the repetition year after year, and looked for ways to amuse himself. This year, as always, he marched back and forth on the edge of the field, stopped to chat with spectators, whistled a favorite tune and, finally, dozed on a park bench.

Suddenly, he was jolted out of his torpor by a cry for help. He looked around and saw a boy being pulled along by his kite. The boy simply could not pull it in. He fell to the ground. People shouted at him to let go, but he seemed determined to hold on. Officer Murphy ran to him as he was being pulled along and grabbed hold of the handle. Finally, the boy let go. Now the kite was pulling Officer Murphy along the ground and gaining speed as it went. He felt the string go taut but somehow managed to keep his grip on the handle. Then he abruptly felt himself lifted into the air and soon he was flying over the heads of the spectators. He rose farther. He could look down and survey the whole town of Upper Chester. It was all so beautiful, he laughed with a glee he had never before experienced.

Of course, that did not last. Officer Murphy began to worry that he might never return to earth. That worry turned into real panic when he felt the string slacken, causing him to go into freefall. He held on tight, as if that would slow his descent. Suddenly something astonishing happened. It was as though the kite took pity on him, swooping down under him and boring him up. It then gently placed him back on the ground.

He stood there in utter amazement. What an extraordinary adventure! He looked around to see where the kite ended up. It was

(sl)

nowhere to be seen. Even the handle and the string had disappeared. In a daze, he stumbled back to the field where he started. He wanted to find the boy who had brought the kite. He would love to ride that magical kite again, but no one was there. Officer Murphy sat on the park bench stunned and in awe. It was as though nothing ever happened there. In the days that followed, he asked people if any of them recalled seeing him lift off from earth and fly. No one did. People began to regard Police Sergeant Brian Murphy as a little peculiar.

The next April, he went again to do his duty, patrolling the grounds for the kite competition. He sat on the bench, hoping the boy would show up with that magical kite for another wondrous flight over the village. It did not happen. Nor did it the following April.

A Boy and His Tree

Young Cyril Desmond Tinker was not the usual playground boy. In fact, he much preferred being alone in the woods. He liked his name and when asked, he would answer with all three: first, middle and last. His schoolmates made fun of him and teased him for being so serious and aloof. He tried not to let it bother him, but it did. In response, he tended to withdraw into his own little world, the world of trees.

In his worldview, trees were stalwart, solid, reliable, and simply beautiful. That applied to all trees, no matter what type. They all stood their ground. He admired that. There were the majestic trees, such as oak, elm, redwood and cedar. Then there were great pine trees and even fruit trees. The one exception was bonsai trees, because he saw them as victims of torture. He thought that, if they could express themselves, they would simply scream.

Cyril Desmond Tinker had one very special tree, a magnificent towering elm tree that stood on a hillside several yards away from the

(cl)

family house. He was enormously fond of that tree, so much so that he felt the need to give it a name. Of course, it had to be as impressive as his own name. He tried out a whole series of names: Englebert, Bertrand, Roland, Frederick, Orlando, and many others. It had to be a good one, because he developed a habit of talking to the tree, and he would like to address it by name. He finally settled on a name. He called the tree "Galahad." He liked the sound of that as he tried it out speaking: "Galahad the Great Elm." He had no idea where he got that name. He just liked it.

Once the tree had a name, a routine developed. After school, Cyril would come home, have a glass of milk and a cookie and then go sit in the shade of Galahad the Great Elm. He'd do this even when it was raining, as Galahad's canopy could keep him dry. On Saturdays and Sundays he'd spend as much time with that tree as he could. Naturally, whenever he felt the need of some comfort, he would return to his friend, Galahad. He sensed the tree understood him in ways no human could – not even his mother or his father. For example, he was very upset when his father scolded him severely for dawdling after school rather than coming straight home, as he should. When his father, at last, turned to other business, he slipped out and went to his tree.

Soon after that, there was another occasion when he needed Galahad for comfort. His mother disappeared for a few days and then came home with a baby. Cyril did not know where that baby came from, but he was told that it was his sister. People fussed over the thing until Cyril could stand it no more. He went out of the house and plopped down at the base of Galahad the Great Elm. He talked to that tree, complaining that everyone cooed and giggled over that crying lump. He felt certain the tree understood. No one else did. Cyril leaned back against the tree trunk and gazed up into its thick canopy overhead.

All was quiet except for the rustling of leaves. Cyril sighed. His eyelids got heavy. After a while, he heard someone say something. He looked all around. There was no one in sight. He settled back down, thinking that it must have been an illusion. It came again. He looked up into the leaves, and this time he heard the words distinctly. The tree was talking. It said, "Don't worry."

"Galahad, are you talking? Is that you?"

"Yes," replied the tree.

"You can talk?"

"Only when you need me to."

"Do I need you to talk now?"

"What do you think?" The tree answered the question with a question.

Cyril thought for a while. It had never occurred to him that he might need his favorite tree to talk to him. After all, this was the very first time the tree had ever talked. Why, it was the first time any tree had talked to him, but then, this was his *very special* tree.

So began a long conversation between the boy and his tree. Cyril described this bawling lump, supposedly his sister. The tree assured him that the lump will change into something he really could call a sister. Cyril responded, saying he didn't ask for a sister. He certainly did not want one. The tree was a good listener, a very understanding one. In a soothing tone, the tree assured Cyril things would get better. The conversation ended abruptly when Cyril heard his father call him to come in for dinner. The boy thanked his tree and ran inside.

In the days that followed, the boy and his tree had other conversations, particularly whenever Cyril was upset or worried. One afternoon, he came home from school and went directly to the tree without stopping for his milk and cookie. He told Galahad the Great Elm about a new pupil in his class, a big, fat bully, named Roscoe. He and his lieutenant, a scrawny boy the other kids called Ichabod, began abusing others on the playground. At first, their favorite tactic was to stand very close on both sides of the victim and taunt him with mocking, sneering remarks. A few days later, they added pushes and shoves. Inevitably, they would spot Cyril Desmond Tinker as a good mark. They started by spewing his full name in high-pitched, snarling voices. Then they decided it was fun to play with his last name, Tinker. "Hey, hey, tinker kid, waddya tink? Betcha can't even tink a tonk." They repeated that one so often that Cyril could quote it through tears. The tree was very upset for the boy. In fact, it responded with intense anger toward Roscoe and Ichabod. A few days later, when he came home weeping after having been thrown to the ground and kicked, the tree reacted with such ferocious passion that Cyril could feel it pulling at its roots. Cyril restrained the tree by telling it that a teacher had stopped the bullying and sent the two to the principal's office.

After being severely disciplined, the two bullies wanted some sort of revenge, as if Cyril were to blame. They found where the Tinkers lived and they let Cyril know they'd come for him. Cyril tried to be vigilant at all times, especially whenever he was alone outside by himself resting at the base of Galahad the Great Elm. As a special safeguard, he enlisted Galahad to keep watch.

One day Cyril felt the earth under him shudder. The tree was pulling at its roots. He saw the bullies were stomping up the hill toward him. Suddenly, he felt a powerful jerk underneath him. The tree yanked itself up by the roots and ran toward them using its roots as feet. The bullies were frozen in amazement as they looked up at the

(sl)

towering Galahad bearing down on them. They tried to run, but it was too late. They fell cowering to the ground. With some satisfaction, Cyril watched the tree use its lower limbs to give them a thorough beating.

After that, Cyril again felt the earth move under him. He turned and saw that the tree was firmly back in the ground. It seemed his tree had replanted itself – or perhaps it had never uprooted itself in the first place. It may have been a dream, but the truth is Roscoe and Ichabod never bothered Cyril Desmond Tinker again.

Sylvie's Flight

Sylvie was mad. She was really mad and she stomped all the way home from the playing field in the city park. A group of boys had gathered there to divide into two baseball teams. When she got there, two boys were choosing their teams. She ran to join the group and waited to hear her name called. She waited, but they did not call her name. She knew they knew her name and she knew their names, too. She called out, "Hey, Sam, what about me? Which team am I on?"

Sam sauntered over to Sylvie. "You're not on any team. You're just a girl. Girls can't play."

Brian joined Sam. With a sneer, he told her, "Girls don't know how to throw a ball or even catch one. Girls are no good."

"I do **too**, know how to throw a ball."

Sam smirked. "Girls throw in a sissy way."

Brian added, "Besides, you're ugly."

Then Brian put his arm around Sam's shoulder and they both laughed. They turned their backs on her and ran to join the others.

Everyone started making hoopla with shouts to power themselves up for the game. Once in a while, one of them would shoot a glaring look at Sylvie standing alone at the edge of the field. That was when Sylvie got mad, **really mad**, so much so that she considered picking up a small rock she found and showing how she could throw. Instead, she turned and, muttering to herself, stomped toward home.

By the time she arrived, her anger began to shift into something very different. She could feel that shift. After all, there was not much she could do with that anger. She sat down on the back porch stoop. She went on muttering, "Why did I have to be a girl? I didn't **ask** to be a girl. I wish I could change myself into something else. I wouldn't be a boy. That's **much** worse. They are always boasting, bragging, swaggering and swearing. They're awful! What's more, they're **ugly**. Yes, they are UGLY!"

She went on in this vein, reassuring herself that, at least, she was pretty. She stopped talking in her head and started looking around the yard. She could hear bees buzzing and birds twittering. She turned and looked at a honeybee flitting among the blossoms of a bush next to the stoop. She looked up and saw a bird soaring on spread wings. In the backyard there was a hammock stretched between two trees. Seeing it reminded her how much comfort it gave her whenever she was sad.

Sylvie climbed into that hammock. It sagged under her weight, enough so that she felt herself wrapped inside of it. It was very comforting, causing her to doze off.

The next thing she knew a large caterpillar was busy gnawing

(cl)

away at the hammock. It went on doing so until Sylvie suddenly felt herself out in the open spreading two beautiful wings with very colorful patterns in white, red, black and orange. She examined herself. She was amazed. The hammock dropped away along with the caterpillar and Sylvie flew up into the trees. From there she could see her house and yard and the street where she lived. She flew over the playing field and out into the countryside. She looked down on farmlands, rivers and a lake, and laughed with delight. It was all simply exhilarating.

Sylvie felt a soft breeze pass over her. She blinked her eyes. For a moment she felt lost, disoriented. Then she recognized the trees overhead and realized she was back home in that comforting hammock. She lay there for a while simply relishing her adventure. To tell anyone about it would somehow spoil it. She kept it to herself. Besides, it was so beautiful she would not be able to find the words to describe it. That evening Sylvie sat at the family dinner table smiling quietly.

The Woman Who Left the Room

Ben Maleon was an artist - a highly successful one. He frequently won lucrative commissions. He was noted for his enormous paintings that adorned foyers of high-rise office buildings. He had hit on a formula for such paintings. It consisted of complex geometric patterns arranged to create the illusion of depth. He was proud of this work, but he was growing tired of the repetitious, almost mechanical, routine. His agent, Peter Larkin, was very effective in securing one commission after another. Ben was pleased, of course, but he had secretly begun to hope for a respite, allowing him to undertake some more fulfilling work.

One evening, as Ben sat looking at a huge half-finished canvas, he decided to do something he hadn't done since his days at the Academy: build a small canvas and paint on it whatever comes to mind. He quickly set about doing that. Once the canvas had been stretched on the frame he had constructed, he went to his storage closet and brought out an easel of appropriate size. He set the canvas on the easel, sat down and stared at it. As he stared, some images began to pass through his mind's eye. They included a grove of trees at sunset, a grotesque face mask, three nudes posed like the Three Graces, a portrait of Christ with his crown of thorns, a horse and rider, a mother and child, some more landscapes. They came tumbling one after another. He closed his eyes, hoping to stop them, but they kept coming. He shook his head, stood up and turned his attention to the great abstract canvas.

At that moment, the phone rang. It was Peter Larkin, wanting to know if Ben was making progress and reminding him that the deadline was fast approaching. The artist, a bit petulantly, assured his agent he was hard at work and hung up. Not long after, he put up his brushes, cleaned his hands and went to bed.

Images kept playing in his head until he fell into a deep slumber. He awoke in the morning with a new image playing before him. Ben forced his eyes to remain shut for fear of losing this new image. He studied it closely. The face of a beautiful woman appeared before him. Her head was turned slightly away, yet she still seemed to look back at him. The image stayed with him even after he rose from his bed. He dressed quickly and, trying hard to maintain that image in his mind, ran into the studio and started preparing his paints and brushes. Keeping the image before him, he went to work transposing it to the white blank canvas. The image faded, but he kept on painting feverishly. The phone rang. He picked it up, declaring he could not talk just then and hung up.

Hours later, Ben stopped, exhausted. He threw himself into a chair

(sl)

and contemplated his creation. The woman looked back askance. "She's beautiful," he thought, but he told himself he hadn't quite gotten her right. Her cheeks needed to be lifted ever so slightly and she should have a smile playing on her lips. He worked intensely on correcting these details and found a few other subtleties to refine. It seemed he spent hours, if not days, perfecting the image, all the while putting off the ever-persistent Peter Larkin. Finally, one night, Ben Maleon threw himself into the chair and looked at her. She was truly beautiful. To do anything more risked ruining that living, vibrant being he had created with mere pigments. He felt drawn to her, mesmerized by her engaging glance. It was all he could do to break his gaze, turn out the lights and retire for the night.

But then he had a second thought. He came back into the studio and turned the lights back on. Without touching her radiant face, he created the room in which she lived. He mixed new paints to use for the walls. It took on a sort of pleasant glow from the sunlight in the window and the red wall tapestries. Ben added a door beyond her right shoulder. He smiled with deep satisfaction. Ben cleaned his brushes and turned to leave. He stopped to look back at her. Then she did something astonishing – or at least he thought she did. She winked. He stood stock-still, anticipating she might do that again. After some time, he shrugged and decided it must have been an illusion. He turned out the lights and left the room.

The next morning, the phone rang. Peter told him he was on his way over now that the deadline was upon them. "All right, all right, come over. I'm not going anywhere." He dressed and went to the studio to see his beloved once again. He set his chair opposite the easel and settled in to commune with his woman.

Suddenly, she pulled back and stood up. She returned his gaze for a brief moment, and then walked to the door. She glanced back with a smile, opened the door and left.

Flabbergasted, Ben Maleon sank down in his chair. The wind had been knocked out of him. He sat there staring at the empty room. There was a knock on the studio door. Ben ignored it and kept on staring. The knocks became louder and more persistent. Ben remained transfixed as he stared at the empty room and the open door.

Peter let himself in. "What in the world are you doing? Are you deaf? You had me out there knocking until my knuckles got red. Have you just been sitting there this whole time? And what are you looking at?" Peter went to the easel. "You've painted a room. Good for you! What got into you to want to paint a room? Have you forgotten your commission? Say something."

Ben continued staring at the empty room.

"Say something, can't you? The deadline is upon us. There in front of us is the painting and clearly it's not ready. What am I supposed to say to our client?" Ben continued staring.

"Are you listening to me? Talk to me!"

Ben turned to him and muttered, "She's gone."

Peter saw that the man had a tear running down his cheek. He immediately changed his tone. "Oh, I am so sorry. It must be hard on you. Who's gone?"

Ben turned back to the canvas. "Went out the door."

Peter was puzzled and remarked, "That's an interesting metaphor."

"Got up and walked out the door."

There was a long pause, neither of them knowing just what to say. Finally, Peter broke the silence. "Well, nothing we can do will bring her back. Listen! You have to get to work. You understand what I'm telling you? Do you?"

Ben nodded and stood up. It took some cajoling, but Peter got him back to work on the commissioned painting. Slowly and methodically, Ben set about mixing his paints. Once Peter saw him begin applying his brush to the canvas, he was satisfied and quietly let himself out.

From that day forward, Ben was never quite able to cast off the face of the woman who left the room. From time to time, he glanced at the painting of the empty room and the open door. She never returned.

An Infernal Misadventure

One day, Oliver Wells lost his wife. It wasn't that he misplaced her. She was there one moment and gone the next. They were seated together in their living room, he in his favorite armchair and she on the couch, when suddenly she blurted out, "It hurts!" She slumped over and was gone. He rushed to her side, held her face in his hands and saw that she was no longer in there. He telephoned for help. A medical team arrived very quickly and went to work trying to revive her. It was no use. The sheriff came and put him through a battery of questions. After a while, the coroner and his team arrived and took her away. Oliver was left alone. He sat on that couch for a very long time. He felt numb, empty.

This was not the plan. He was supposed to go first. He hadn't been feeling well for some time. It was nothing alarming, just a general sense of weariness and ennui. He liked to say he was having "intimations of mortality." Nevertheless, she went ahead without a hint of warning.

After her passing, he took to muttering things to himself, things such as "I'm so tired" or "I want to go home." He wondered what "home" was. He thought about it continually. "Perhaps," he thought, "it referred to a place prepared for me in the Afterlife." In any event, he decided he ought to make good use of what time he had left in this life. He took up a program of reading and he planted a garden, but most of all he went on excursions, listened to concerts, attended plays, and toured exhibitions.

This eventually led him to visit the city's museum of fine art. He recalled several works of art he would like to see again. One was a painting from the late eighteenth century, a portrait of a woman with a haunting look, made all the more so by her eyes that seemed to follow wherever you moved. Another was a Renaissance marble statue of a dejected man seated on a rock with his elbows on his knees. It was labeled "Esau." Oliver thought he understood the poor man. But the one exhibit he most wanted to see consisted of frescoes pulled from the walls of a medieval church that had fallen into disuse. He went as directly as possible, passing the gaze of the lady, until he came to a rotunda where those frescoes were on display.

Oliver planted himself on a bench facing a huge depiction of the Last Judgment. Not only was the painting large, it was crowded. There were angels flitting about on high, little dark devils scurrying among scattered lost souls, confused and wandering in many directions, some just pulling themselves out of their graves. To the left side was a golden gate behind a great desk at which Saint Peter was working on the Book of Life. On the other side stood a grotesque monster with a gaping

(sl)

mouth. Finally, at the center of all this mayhem stood the magnificent figure of the Archangel Michael placing souls, one at a time, on his scales to test their weight against a dead weight on the other side.

Oliver studied all this activity. He became engrossed in it, even mesmerized by it. After a while, as Oliver was nodding off, the picture started coming to life. His sleep turned frenetic, causing him to rock his body and wave his arms. The devils chased some of the souls out of the painting, onto the museum floor. They snatched up souls and hauled them back into the painting where Michael could catch them and put them one by one on his scales. He gave the heavy ones over to the devils who dragged them into the monster's mouth; others, the lighter ones, went to Peter's desk.

Then something amazing happened: a devil jumped out of the picture, ran to Oliver, and forced him into the painting, next to Michael. The moment Michael put Oliver on the scales, the devil reached up and pulled Oliver's side of the scale down. Michael declared him too heavy and gave him over to the devil. The devil made a shout and dragged Oliver over to Hell's Mouth. He threw Oliver straight into that mouth. At that moment, something even stranger occurred. The painting shifted to that side, revealing the monster's gullet, where Oliver could be seen swallowed up by the monster and falling. The devil, being heavier, passed him by and of course landed first.

Oliver landed and immediately jumped to his feet. He was furious. He ran to the devil shouting, "You bastard! I know what you have done. With just a yank on those scales you made me appear heavy with sin. And now you have me in this murky underground world. You've destroyed my promised home in Heaven."

With a smirk, the devil answered him quietly. "Calm yourself. Easy does it. Things aren't nearly so bad. For starters, this place is much more interesting. Up in Heaven, every day forever and ever, you would be singing choral chants, flitting about among the clouds with your wings, and then singing again…day after day after day, for all time."

Oliver snorted, "Hah, and here I suppose you happen to have some truly entertaining tortures that come in endless variety."

The devil responded, "Let me show you. I believe you are Oliver Wells. My name's Todeotus and I will be serving as your guide here in Hell for the next few thousand years. I assure you, it is all amazing. You'll enjoy my tour. I'll take you into all nine circles of Hell. You'll find it fascinating. You'll be enthralled. Give me a chance to show you."

Then Todeotus suddenly turned and looked down the steep hill to the banks of the swirling waters of a misty river. "We'll need to get down there right away. Charon's ferry is about to come into dock. He'll take us across the River Styx to the starting point of our tour. Come!" They ran down the hill and, just as predicted, an open barge appeared. Crowds of anxious souls were gathered like a herd being pushed and shoved onto the boat. Oliver watched the proceedings with distaste. He saw the ferryman pushing souls this way and that, and sometimes using an oar to beat the recalcitrant ones who hung back. Oliver turned away, saying, "They can go ahead without me."

"No, no. You can't stay here. I'll make sure Charon treats you well. Now, come this way."

Reluctantly, Oliver went on board with Todeotus, who introduced the ferryman. Charon, for his part, warmly welcomed Oliver on board his ship and found him a comfortable place to sit. Then the boat moved out into the currents of the river and through the mists rising out of its warm waters.

Once they were well out into the middle of that mighty river, Oliver noticed a thin ray of light. The ray grew larger until it was a full shaft of light pouring through a great hole overhead. Out of that hole emerged an angel, flapping wings and descending straight to Oliver. Once the angel was almost face to face with him, Oliver heard the words, "Sir. Do you hear me? Are you all right?"

Oliver blinked his eyes and saw a woman's beautiful face before him. She repeated, "Are you all right? Do you need help?" Then he heard another voice saying, "Look, lift him up and put him on the floor. Maybe we can bring him around." Oliver then felt himself being lifted, but it became a very different sensation for him. He sensed himself being carried aloft by the angel into that shaft of light and on through the bright hole above.

Todeotus watched Oliver's soul soaring up and vanishing into the bright hole. He watched it all in great astonishment until the hole closed up. Although he had heard of this sort of event, he had never seen it happen. There was one time that everyone in Hell still talks about when a shaft of light pulled thousands of souls out of Hell and through a bright hole, but that was more than two thousand years ago.

As soon as the bright hole closed up, Todeotus felt himself yanked back into the fresco to join with his fellow devils. Meanwhile, the medical team, unaware of what had just happened, worked on Oliver's body.

Thwarting Apollo's Lust

The river god, Peneus, had become a curmudgeon. It was a matter of bitter attitude rather than old age. The gods, after all, don't age and die, although some seem to be eternally old. Peneus had lost the zest he used to feel and it bothered him to see gods and goddesses gamboling about in an unending game of love and chance. It annoyed him enough to cause him to growl and curse whenever he encountered a pair on his riverbank wrapped in loving arms. If that did not drive them away, he had some conjuring powers. For example, he would create an owl that would swoop down on them or he would cause a waterspout from the river to douse the lovers. Lovers knew to avoid the river where he resided. Those who did not, soon learned.

There was a particular god who stuck in his craw. It was Apollo, god of light, music, and all the arts, with the stable of muses he kept on Mount Parnassus. He was also handsome, admired by goddesses and nymphs, whom he enjoyed seducing. All of that made Peneus

(cl)

gnash his teeth and scheme for ways to expose Apollo to ridicule and embarrassment.

Peneus had a daughter. Her name was Daphne, and she appeared young and beautiful. This worried him, as it was just a matter of time before Apollo would notice her. He warned her repeatedly to ignore his sweet words. He made sure that she knew Apollo only wanted to use her. In short, he planted fear in her about him and all other male gods. It was of some comfort to him that Daphne was lithe and fleet of foot.

On a pleasant afternoon, Peneus was napping on his riverbank when he heard what sounded like a cry for help. He shook his head awake and listened. The cry came again, this time it was recognizable. He stood and looked in the direction of the voice.

It was Daphne, and he saw her running full-tilt. He climbed to the top of the riverbank. Her speed was impressive. Then he saw Apollo in close pursuit, gradually gaining ground.

Peneus knew he had to act quickly. He had to do something. It had to be something that would not only stop Apollo but also so stymie him as to leave him exposed to ridicule. He had a magical trick in his conjuring repertoire. He cast the power of that trick out to Daphne just as Apollo was reaching to hold her. Suddenly, she began to turn into a

(cl)

tree. Apollo grabbed hold of what he thought was her waist. Instead he held onto her trunk. Instead of touching her soft flesh, he held her tree bark. She had thrown her arms up and they branched out into many limbs and leaves. Apollo was stunned. He fell to the ground, where he felt tree roots spreading out under him. He was out of breath and the shock of it all made it harder to get it back. He sat there examining his rough hands, and looking up into the tree.

This was just what Peneus wanted, although it would've been better if a crowd of people could see him and mock him. He might do it himself. So, he sauntered over to the poor fellow. "Had a bit of a shock, did you?"

Apollo just stared at him. "Thought you were going to have some fun with her?" Apollo stared at him still. "It's a beautiful laurel tree, isn't it? I guess you can't do much with a tree, however beautiful it is."

Apollo pushed him aside and walked off. "Go on," cried Peneus. "See if you can find another tree to love."

With that, Peneus smiled smugly and sat down at the base of the tree. After a short while, he heard a muffled voice: "Get me out of this." At first, he believed it was an illusion. He hadn't actually heard the tree talk. Suddenly, it struck him that Daphne was in that tree. It was her voice he had heard. It was all his doing. Now he must undo what he had done. He became terribly upset because he could not think of a spell that would work. He couldn't just conjure in reverse. He knew that. His mind flipped through his full repertoire. He could think of nothing that could liberate a woman encased in a tree. The voice in the tree cried out,

"You have to help me, Father. I can't go on being a tree. I just can't."

Peneus was frantic, "I'm trying! I'm trying!" And he **was** trying, but every attempt resulted in something useless, even absurd. At one point, he conjured another tree, a duplicate of the laurel tree that encased Daphne, but without Daphne. Frustrated and angry, he tried that spell again, only to create a grove of laurel trees. Another attempt caused the tree to lose its leaves, exposing Daphne to view, her arms and fingers still extending out into branches.

"That's no good. I'm still stuck in this tree," she said.

Disheartened, Peneus sat down at the base of the tree where he held his face in his hands. It happened that Apollo was at that moment strolling in the laurel grove, where he had woven a wreath to adorn his head. He looked up and saw Peneus in that abject posture. He smiled.

After a moment, he approached the poor god. "Problem?" he asked. Peneus did not move. "It seems you have your daughter up a tree." He chuckled at his little joke. Peneus still did not move.

Daphne did move, shaking her branches. "Help me!'

Apollo showed his concern with her distress, saying, "I would love to help you and I think I can. A woman of your charm and beauty should never be trapped in this way."

"Did you say you could help me get out of this tree? Could you really do that?'

Peneus looked up. Apollo smiled at him: "I seem to recall your saying something like 'I guess you can't do much with a tree, however beautiful it is.' The fact is I can do something with this tree."

"Oh, please. Please do!" exclaimed Daphne.

Peneus quietly murmured, "I would be much obliged."

"Would you now?"

"I beg you, forgive me. Don't let her suffer another minute."

Apollo smirked, "Then stand aside." Peneus did as he was told. Then Apollo created a great shaft of light to land on Daphne. Her arms and fingers loosened from the branches. The leaves jumped back in place and the bark fell away from the tree trunk. Daphne stepped out.

She stood facing Apollo for a moment, and then threw her arms around him in a tight embrace. He responded, stroking her back. Eventually, they broke the embrace, smiled at one another and walked off together, leaving Peneus desolate and ashamed.

A Romp in a Golden Sea

Anthony and Eleanor sought every kind of pleasant setting where they could be alone to indulge in each other. They found such places in a rowboat on a beautiful lake, on the observation deck of a skyscraper, on a mountainside above a cable car stop, and even in an abandoned movie theater.

The most unusual experience they shared occurred while they were enjoying a picnic on a gentle grassy slope above an enormous wheat field. The golden stalks of wheat extended far into the distance. Eleanor had found that spot and suggested it was ideal for a picnic. They packed a basket full of fruits, sandwiches and some Chardonnay. A balmy breeze caressed them as they finished the bottle and relaxed into each other's arms.

The breeze gradually developed into a wind. It was not strong, but strong enough to cause Eleanor to sit up.

"Look," she said. "Look! See how the wind creates ripples in the wheat. It makes the wheat look like water."

"Umph," said Anthony as he nuzzled the nape of her neck.

"No, really. Look. It's amazing."

"Umph," he repeated, being otherwise occupied.

The wind down on the field had become stronger, turning the ripples into waves.

"Stop that, Tony. You have to see this."

He tried to get her to lie down, but she resisted and suddenly called out, "Wait, wait. What is that? There's something down there and it's really big!"

He smiled proudly. "You noticed!"

She became insistent and pushed him away. "Tony, I mean it. Look down on the field, will you? What is that enormous thing plowing through the wheat?"

At last, Anthony looked out on the field. He opened his eyes wide, not believing what he was seeing. They both stared in sheer astonishment. "It looks like a great serpent, its head and long neck standing above the wheat."

"Yes! Like a sea serpent! And it's not plowing, it's swimming. Look how it leaves a wake. The wheat seems to have turned into golden water, and the waves are tumbling onto the edge of the field."

"Yes. And the edge has become a shore," he added.

By then, the serpent had dived out of sight. The two ran down the hill to the shore, hoping to see it surface again. As soon as they got there, the golden water built up into a tremendous towering wave and crashed over them. They were pulled out into the sea. There they thrashed about, caught up in a desperate fear. It seemed certain they were about

(cl)

to drown, if not be devoured by the serpent, whose whereabouts they couldn't guess.

Something else happened, as astonishing as what had gone before. This golden water was different. It had enough substance to mount up into a wave and enough resistance to buoy you up, but it also allowed you to breathe as if it were air. There was no chance of drowning. Meanwhile, Anthony and Eleanor admired crystalline bubbles, whirling around them like little spheres of topaz. In sheer delight, the lovers gamboled about in playful joy.

They realized in a rush that the serpent must still be somewhere in this golden sea. They scrambled to get to the shore, fighting against the surf. In the midst of their struggle, they turned and saw, to their horror, the serpent right behind them. Trapped, they stared at the creature, convinced that this was the end. Instead, they saw a smile develop on the serpent's face. It was not a smile of triumph, rather an engaging smile that invited playfulness. Indeed, the three romped about in the golden bubbles.

Suddenly, without warning, the serpent disappeared, the golden water transformed into wheat, and Anthony and Eleanor fell to the ground among the stalks. They lay there exhausted. They looked at one another and laughed quietly. The golden water was gone, leaving them dry. Finally, Anthony got up and helped her to her feet, saying, "That was *some* ride!" They dusted themselves off and made their way out of the field and up the hill. From that day, they marveled about what had happened, never quite sure if it was real. If not, this may be one of those times when illusion is more powerful than reality.

The Empress Issues a Death Sentence

Rupert Alan Pomeroy was a very busy man who worked in the financial district of a big city. His work pleased him because he had a knack for manipulating accounts by withdrawing funds from one investment and placing them in another. He told himself that these transactions benefitted clients all over the country. He was not altogether wrong in thinking in this way, but the real source of his pleasure was the power he felt as he built up or tore down whole businesses. (That power may not have been real, but it pleased him to think so.)

What detracted from that pleasure was his deep dislike for the city. Walking through the streets of the city literally set his teeth on edge. Indeed, he had dental problems that came from grinding his teeth as he made his way through the throngs of people darting this way and that and bunching up at every red light. For that reason, he bought a house in the quiet suburbs. It meant, however, he had to start early in the morning to find parking at the train station and catch the 7:40 into the city. Even then, he had to make his way through the crowds from the Central Metropolitan Rail Station to the offices of his firm. In compensation, the routine afforded him the chance to nap going in and coming back out. In his downtime at home, he liked gardening, even though he was having trouble lately with anthills. No sooner would he manage to destroy one hill, then he would find another one mounting up nearby.

One day, as he made his way through the crowds, he realized that he had been witnessing a strange event repeated over and over. Men wearing black overalls came to the edge of a hole in the pavement and disappeared, climbing down a ladder inside. To make it even stranger, he never saw anyone climb out of that hole. Those men disappeared, but never reappeared. On this particular day, he went to the edge of the hole and looked down. He could see nothing in that darkness, but he sensed great commotion. He could not guess what might be happening, so he went on to his office.

The next morning, after a fitful night, he overslept and had to rush to pull himself together and make a dash for the 7:40. Fortunately, the train was ten minutes late and it arrived just as he stepped onto the platform. Rupert climbed on board and sank into a seat with a sigh of relief. It was very warm in the railway car and he regretted putting on his woolen sweatshirt. That and the rocking motion of the train soon lulled him into sleep. Not even the occasional stops along the way to the city caused him to awaken.

As he slept, he dreamt he went to the edge of that hole. The commotion piqued his curiosity and this time he decided to climb down the ladder and find out what it was all about. As soon as he got to the last rung of the ladder, he felt each elbow being grabbed by someone. He then was ushered into an open circular area. To his horror, he noticed he was completely surrounded by giant ants. The two at his elbows were ants as tall as himself when they stood on their hind legs.

Then he heard a strange voice call out his name in a chopping, clipped way. "Rupert Alan Pomeroy!" He turned and saw a giant ant seated on a throne. That regal ant was draped in an ermine boa, wore a crown and held a scepter. Rupert realized why the voice was so choppy: the words were spoken through the ant's powerful mandibles.

(sl)

Those same words came clattering out again: "Are you Rupert Alan Pomeroy?" Rupert swallowed hard. "Yes." The voice barked, "You are to address me as Your Imperial Highness." "Yes, ma'am." There was a heavy silence. Finally, he caught on: "Yes, Your Imperial Highness." Things were not looking good for Rupert. The voice continued, "I am the Empress of Formicea and all its colonies. Do you understand?"

"Yes, Your Imperial Highness."

After a suitable pause, the voice continued. "Then let us attend to the business at hand. You, Rupert Alan Pomeroy, stand accused of the crime of mass murder. Evidence shows you have destroyed eight of our Formicean colonies and their entire populations. We are not pleased. How do you plead?"

"Not guilty, Your Imperial Highness."

"You have to be kidding, Rupert Alan Pomeroy. You know full well that you destroyed all those colonies. The evidence is incontrovertible. Now what do you have to say?"

"I don't know."

"You don't know…WHAT?"

Rupert gulped. "I don't know, Your Imperial Highness."

"Guilty as charged," announced the Empress. "**Chew. Him. Up.**"

In response, all the surrounding ants descended on him and began mercilessly biting and stinging him. They were even tearing off bits of flesh and carrying them away.

The conductor saw Rupert twisting and squirming in his woolen sweatshirt. He tapped him on the shoulder and asked "Sir, are you all right? Do you need help? Can you hear me?" Rupert woke up with a start. He looked around wildly, still waving his arms and legs in the air.

He slowly calmed down. He looked about. People were staring at him with some alarm. The conductor said, "You had me worried there for a while. It seemed you might need some medical intervention. But now I believe you were simply having a bad dream."

Rupert shook his head to clear himself of the horror of that dream. "I was being eaten alive."

The conductor nodded and the other passengers settled back in their seats. Rupert took in a long breath. The train was coming into the station and he gathered his belongings and waited for it to come to a complete stop. When he emerged from the Central Metropolitan Rail Station, he started out in the direction of his office building. This time, rather than striding while grinding his teeth, he strolled along, allowing all the others to swirl around him.

After some time, of course, he came to that hole. This time there was a man in black overalls putting up a sign, warning pedestrians to stay clear of danger. Rupert went up to him and inquired, "What's going on down in that hole?" He found out that workers were going down that ladder to repair a leak in the water main at this point and then on to another leak farther on. There the workers could climb out a nearby manhole. "Ah," muttered Rupert, "that's why I never saw anyone climb out of this hole. Now I understand." He turned and continued his stroll toward his office. It was a pleasant morning with a soft cool breeze. Now it felt good to have on that woolen sweatshirt.

The dream had had a strange effect on him. Ever after that, he slowed his pace and savored his life. He even enjoyed studying the faces of the people rushing by him. Back home in the suburbs he enjoyed gardening more than ever. It scarcely need be said that he never disturbed an anthill again.

Repairs and Replacement Parts

*I*t would seem a blessing to arrive at the age of eighty after a full life. One can relish rich and satisfying memories of people and places. Images in photos and written words in journals and letters can spark the reliving of it all. Of course, there are gaps from time to time when memory can't quite conjure a former time. There are also times when one cannot trust a memory and wonder, "Did that really happen?"

All that is true for Seymor Smollett, but often the blessing is a mixed one. There are always those regrets that come with memories, times when he missed an opportunity or times when he could not forgive himself for having harmed someone. Beyond those experiences out of the past are the aches and pains of the present.

Seymor Smollett lived in a cottage on the edge of a small town. He lived there for forty-three years with his wife, Ingrid, whose death left him alone the last five years. Her death brought on a grief he could never shake off.

From these aches, pains, regrets, and grief, Seymor looked for relief. A book, a letter, or a photo would renew the sadness. There was no one available with whom he could make amends for his regrets. He decided, however, that he could do something about the aches and pains. He joined a club to work out and launched a regimen of exercise. He took long walks. He would walk for miles, from early morning to noon. Sometimes he would add another walk at sunset. He was determined to make his body strong and resilient. He found an added benefit in the simple act of observing the world he passed through. He saw birds flitting from branch to branch, ants hauling things to their anthill home, flowers and trees moving with the breeze, clouds scudding across the sky.

All that walking and exercising did pay dividends. He felt stronger and certainly healthier. After some time, however, it began to add to his aches and pains. There was no denying it. Arthritis caused the toes on his left foot to curl under, creating new pain. His right hip went just slightly out of joint. He found he could not breathe quite so easily. There were park benches along the way, and he began to use them.

One day, Seymor Smollett settled into one of those benches to catch his breath. He noticed a low-lying brick building across the street. He must have passed by it many times, but this time something about that building made him curious. The sign on top of the building read "Repairs and Replacement Parts." It looked like a garage, yet there were no automobiles there. Seymor surmised that it must have gone out of business, leaving the place empty. He thought he could use some repairs

(sl)

and replacement parts. He chuckled about that thought and started to resume his walk, favoring his right foot, when he heard someone call his name. He looked back and saw a small man in a white coat standing at the door to the low brick building.

The man repeated, "Mr. Smollett?"

Seymor was puzzled. "Do I know you?"

"No, you don't know me." The man walked over to Seymor and looked up into his face. "But I do know you." He paused for a moment, then began to list the many things he knew about Seymor Smollett, all those regrets and his grief. He listed some of the events in Seymor's life, where he lived, how he met a woman and how he married her. He even knew that she had died. He ended by saying, "I've been waiting for a chance to meet you."

Seymor was dumbfounded with this litany of facts, all of which were accurate. He looked at this strange little man without saying a word, waiting to decide what to say. Finally, he asked, "Well then, who are you?"

The little man smiled. "Do forgive me. I should have introduced myself at the start. I am Manny Throckmorton. Doctor Manny Throckmorton, founder and director of AEM, Advanced Experimental Medicine."

Seymor Smollett was beginning to be annoyed. He sat down on his park bench. He looked little Dr. Throckmorton in the eye and said in no uncertain terms, "I don't know how you came by all that personal information about me, but I don't see where you get the right to know it at all."

"I derive that right from my dedication to the betterment of humanity."

"And you conduct that noble cause under a sign that reads, Repairs and Replacement Parts, do you?"

"Yes." Dr. Throckmorton smiled.

"An automotive body and repair shop?"

"Right! Only we're talking about human bodies and replacement parts. Here, let me show you what I mean." The little man, Doctor of AEM, ran into the building.

Seymor Smollett waited on his bench. Eventually, the little doctor reappeared, carrying a large piece of paper, longer than he was tall. He spread it out on the ground in front of the bench. The outline of a human body showed certain parts marked in various colors.

The toes of the left foot and the right hip were colored red. The lungs were colored yellow. The brain was blue. Dr. Throckmorton explained that the red indicated pain in the toes and in the hip, the yellow referred to difficulty in breathing, and the blue, memory loss, regrets and grief. The doctor turned to Seymor and said in a triumphant tone, "Now that's pretty accurate, wouldn't you say?"

Seymor nodded.

"Shall I fix those things?"

"You can do that?"

"Yes, I can. Well, not the regrets and the grief. I cannot touch those. You'll have to deal with them yourself. But I can relieve you of the other problems: memory loss, breathing, hip adjustment and toe pain."

Seymor was skeptical. "How?"

Dr. Throckmorton described a wonderful machine that he would pass over Seymor's body slowly and expel every pain or malfunction he had.

Seymor was even more dubious: "You want to send me through a tight dark tunnel, don't you? I won't do it."

"No. It's nothing like that. I call it my OCD, short for Omnibus Cure Device. It's a handheld instrument that I pass over your body. You'll be amazed how well and how fast it works."

(sl)

Another thought came to mind: "Ah, I suppose it costs an arm and a leg, right?"

"That's an interesting way to put it, but I assure you it won't cost a penny. It's free. I'm here for the betterment of all humanity."

Seymor considered this and finally consented to the procedure, but insisted that he would not enter the brick building.

"Very good," the little doctor said. "We'll do it right here at your bench." Then he ran into the building and brought out a large weird instrument, heavy enough to require two hands. He proceeded to use it, walking around and around Seymor's body in a downward spiral, but stopping at his feet.

Seymor felt it all very odd as he watched the little doctor cycle downward. Then he asked, "All right. Are you done now?"

"No, not quite. Still have to do something about those toes." He ran into the building with his OCD and promptly reappeared with a strange little box, which he set on the ground, calling it his Part Replacement Machine, or PRM. He instructed Seymor to remove his left shoe and sock and put the foot into the box. He obeyed with some hesitation. He felt a pull on his toes and then a tickling sensation. The doctor pulled the box away, reached in and pulled out two misshapen, twisted toes. "There," he declared. "I have replaced your toes." Saying that, he took the PRM and ran back into the building.

Seymor, left by himself and dizzy from the doctor's whirlwind of activity, stood for some moments. He looked down and admired his new toes. He put on his sock and shoe and resumed his walk. His foot, his hip and his breathing did seem improved. He also suddenly remembered a person's name he had earlier been unable to call up. Perhaps even his memory was working better.

The next morning, he determined to maintain his regimen. He looked forward to finding Dr. Throckmorton at the low brick building. As he approached the building, he saw an astounding sight. He came to a full stop, startled to see the doors open to three bays where mechanics were busy repairing cars. No doubt, they were also replacing parts on some cars.

Seymor Smollett popped down heavily on the park bench. He was dumbfounded. He was certain he had never seen people in the low brick building working on cars. He sat there for a long while. He noticed one of the mechanics come out to put some parts in a trash barrel. Seymor waved him to come over. The man wiped his greasy hands on an old cloth and asked what he could do for him.

Seymor took his time. "Do you happen to know a gentleman named Doctor Throckmorton?"

"Nope. Can't say as I do."

"Doctor Manny Throckmorton? He used this place as a sort of medical clinic."

"This place?"

"Yes. He was here yesterday."

"Ya got me. This place been closed for vacation last two weeks." The mechanic shook his head and went back into the building.

Seymor tried to catch his breath. He rose to continue his walk. He felt a slight hitch in his right hip and a sudden sharp pain in the second and third toes on his left foot. He looked back at the sign above the low brick building, muttered to himself and moved on.

Percival's Many Personalities

(Suggested by a story by Marcel Aymé)

Percival Gilcrest was a precise man. He dressed formally, as
if he belonged to a different century. He wore a high collar
with a wide tie, a vest with a pocket watch and chain, and
a coat and hat to top it off. He left for work at the very same hour each
day and returned to his little apartment at a fixed hour. He prepared his
dinners with menus for each day of the week, one for Monday, another
for Tuesday, and so on. He kept his apartment scrupulously clean: "a
place for everything and everything in its place." On Sundays, he varied
this routine slightly by going to the Metro Concert Hall for symphonies,
concertos and string quartets. He was a self-sufficient gentleman.

All this rigor in his habits and dress may have derived from a
quirk in his personality. He had no idea how it originated. He only
became aware of it when he was in his late teens. It frightened him and
he did everything he could to keep it in check. Percival Gilcrest had the
extraordinary power to walk through walls. The first time he found

himself on the other side of a wall was shocking and embarrassing. He did not want it to happen again. On that occasion, he was in the dormitory shower when he heard two big claps of thunder. He knew he had to get out of the shower, but he had gotten soap in his eyes and had become disoriented. He turned this way and that and walked through the wall into the hallway. It was a Sunday, when many visitors were about. He could hear them snicker. Someone screamed. When he finally could see where he was, it did not occur to him that he might walk back through that wall and so he rushed through the gathering to the shower door. Later that day, he passed through a number of walls just to figure out what had happened. For a while, it amused him, and he used it for schoolboy pranks, but then it began to worry him.

He had no idea where this power came from. He certainly did not ask for it. He thought back to what might have produced this phenomenon. The only possibility he could think of was that heavy thunderstorm with great bolts of lightning. Perhaps electricity had something to do with it. Whatever the cause, it unnerved him and he tried to avoid any temptation to walk through a wall. He was left hoping it would go away.

Thereafter, he developed a new personality. He was rigorously focused and determined. He would brook no behavior that was in any way trivial or playful. He charted a career for himself that he expected would project an air of dignity. In college, he took courses in the business school dealing with accounting, economics, organization, and government regulation. In short, he trained as a bureaucrat and emerged as the epitome of the type. Moreover, his co-workers regarded him with some awe, seeing how thoroughly methodical he was. He made elaborate use of analyses, diagrams and flowcharts. He had no close friends and he preferred it that way.

He went to work for an organization called the "Registry and Control of National Labor, Statistical Branch." It suited him very well. He was able to answer letters from legislators and bureau chiefs in beautifully oblique terms. They were authoritative and precise and just persuasive enough to make recipients nod their heads in agreement.

Nathaniel Rosen, the Director of the Registry, was quite pleased to let him carry on in this manner. Everyone was satisfied. Mr. Rosen himself had only the dimmest notion of what Mr. Gilcrest did, but it seemed to bother no one and it kept the man very busy. "Let sleeping dogs lie," he told himself.

The time came, however, for Mr. Rosen to retire. He had a comfortable pension and was pleased to step down. He said farewell to his staff, wishing them well. He made a point of congratulating Mr. Gilcrest for his steady devotion to his work and loyalty to the spirit of the Office. The staff all stood and applauded. He waved and was gone.

Naturally, there had to be a new Director of the Registry Office, and within three days, the role was filled by a certain Charles P. Hewitt. He brought with him a stern commitment to order. He made a point of interviewing each clerk by turns in order to gain full understanding of his or her duties. As the process continued, he made notes on possible re-organization, determined to run a tight ship.

The time came for Percival Gilcrest to come to the Director's office. With a cold smile, Mr. Hewitt invited the poor man to take a seat opposite the desk. He rifled through papers, becoming more and more puzzled as he went. Eventually, he looked up and said, "Tell me, Mr. Gilcrest, what exactly do you DO?"

Percival Gilcrest sat up straight in his chair. "I fulfill an important function of the Registry Office by maintaining a responsive posture vis-à-vis the various bureaus within the organizational structure of our company. Moreover, it falls to me to do whatever is needed in the way of public relations, putting forth, as it were, periodic written accounts of our progress. From time to time, I also carry out correspondence with specific people within our organization and outside in the public sphere."

Mr. Hewitt stared blankly at Mr. Gilcrest. There was an uncomfortable pause. Then he held up a piece of paper. "Is this an example of the work you do?" He began to read: "With reference to your esteemed letter of the fourteenth day of February last, and bearing in mind also our exchange of the previous month, I have the honor of communicating to you that our records contain a clear chronological summary of the Auslander Project that can be made available to you if requested through the usual channels as outlined by the Office of Legal Affairs…"

"And so on…and on. This is your work?"

"Yes."

"But what does it mean? Can you translate it?

"Translate?"

"Yes! It seems to say: 'We have a record of the Auslander Project and you may request it.' Why not have done with it?"

From that time on, things got worse with the new Director. Eventually, he demoted the man and assigned him an office in an old storage nook next to the Director's suite. Percival was naturally very upset. Night and day he calculated ways to retaliate. He remembered his ability to pass through walls. Surely that could provide him with the means of revenge.

Percival set about putting his power to work. The wall between his nook and the Director's suite afforded him a fine occasion. He decided to use it. He planned a wonderful surprise. He put a chair against the wall and stood on it. Then he began to pass through, but stopped just as his head came out the other side. There he was like a trophy animal, his head high on the wall opposite the Director's desk. The Director was working at his desk when he became aware something had happened. He looked around in puzzlement. Seeing nothing, he went back to work. Then he thought he heard a sound from up high. He looked up. Mr. Gilcrest smiled down on him. Mr. Hewitt was thrown back in his chair. He jumped up, ran out of the room and over to the nook. He burst in and found Mr. Gilcrest calmly at work at his little desk. Mr. Hewitt stared at him for a moment and went back to his office.

Pleased with the result of that first attempt, Percival looked for more opportunities, always making sure that Mr. Hewitt was alone when he made appearances through a wall. Once he put only his ear through the wall. Another time, he presented his arms and hands. He appeared at the urinal in the staff restroom. He thought of presenting his buttocks through a wall, but put the thought aside. He went on making strange appearances. Mr. Hewitt became more and more unhinged, losing all sense of mental balance. Eventually he alarmed everyone on the staff, who called in the emergency crews. Mr. Hewitt was taken away to the asylum.

Left behind, Percival cast about for other uses for his walk-through powers. One idea appealed to him, for it was a way to get rich quickly. He checked on the walls of the local bank and determined how to pass through into bank vaults. He marveled at how swiftly he passed through, filled his pockets with bank notes and left. So pleased was he with this success that he repeated the operation with three other banks. In every case he could not contain himself and had to provide a signature. He signed

(sl)

himself as "The Phantom." People naturally wanted to know who the Phantom was and how he managed his heists.

It was a major topic of conversation back at the Registry Office. Percival enjoyed listening to all their theories about the Phantom and how he managed get into the vaults and take out so much booty. After a while he could stand it no more and blurted out, "You want to know who the Phantom is? I will tell you. I am the Phantom."

"YOU?" they repeated

"Yes. I am the Phantom and I have special powers that let me get in and out of bank vaults as I please."

"Special powers? You?" They all looked at one another and burst into laughter. "Special powers!"

He went away and sulked in his nook. That evening he went to a jewelry store. It was closed for the night, but he simply passed through the wall. He smashed some display cases, wrote his signature "Phantom" and waited for the silent alarm to alert the authorities. Soon the night watchman appeared with a police officer. They arrested him and took him to the jail where he was photographed and locked up. His picture appeared in the next issue of the Daily News. Being in jail was no problem. The news ought to convince those back at the Registry that he was indeed the Phantom. He walked out early the next morning – but not before filching the warden's gold watch and leaving it in his jail cell.

Back in the world, he changed out of his elegant clothing and adopted a new identity with a fake moustache, a loud T-shirt, jeans and sandals. That night, he slipped into the Registry and picked up his belongings. Meanwhile, the warden, red faced with anger and embarrassment, ordered a contingent to track down the prisoner. Percival himself watched their comings and goings as he sat at a sidewalk cafe.

Percival noticed a beautiful young woman seated at an adjacent table. She seemed troubled and preoccupied. He grew curious about her and eventually he approached her and asked if he could join her at the table. She nodded. He offered to buy her a coffee. She shook her head. He hesitated, and then sat down. For a while, neither one spoke. Little by little, Percival got her to tell her story. She explained that her husband controlled every facet of her life, except those mornings when he was at work. That allowed her to step out, do the shopping and breathe fresh air. She had to make his lunch after which he napped and then locked her in the bedroom so no man could get to her. Now, Percival (who could walk through walls) was interested. Nevertheless, he told himself to be wary. It could be a scam. It may be that she knew about his special power and planned to trap him somehow.

They conversed for a long while until he became convinced that she did not know about his power. They met again on those occasions when she was at liberty to leave the apartment. He revealed his special powers. She revealed the fact that her husband regularly made overnight, out-of-town trips. These revelations led to their agreeing that he slip through the wall to her bedroom at the next opportunity.

The time came for their amorous meeting. Percival started out for her apartment house as dark clouds were gathering. He could hear distant thunder and pulled his coat around his shoulders. It began to rain big drops. Before he arrived, there was a flash and a crack of thunder. As he passed through the outer wall of the apartment house, he sensed a little resistance. There was another crack of thunder. He approached the wall to her bedroom. This time he had to overcome a much stronger resistance, so strong that he could not get out the other side. Nor could he go back. He called out, but his voice went nowhere. He was trapped, stuck in that wall.

On her side of the wall, she felt terribly disappointed. He must have changed his mind or the storm caused a change of plan. There's time, she thought, for them to make another assignation. They can get to know each other better in the days to come. She turned over and drifted off to sleep.

The Mystery of the Transparent People

One Sunday afternoon, the people of the small town of Muellenberg were out for a stroll, enjoying the bright sunshine and gentle breezes. One group was engaged in animated conversation when one of them suddenly stopped. Of course, everyone stopped with her. Very slowly, she asked, "Did anyone see what I just saw?" They looked at one another. "What did you just see?"

"I just saw a man run by. I tell you, the man was completely transparent."

A young fellow smirked and asked, "If he was so transparent, how did you manage to see him?" That caused a gentle chuckle.

"No, no, really. I could see him and I also could see right through him!"

Others shook their heads. The group went on.

A short time later, a couple, strolling through the city park, stopped in front of a bench where they saw a man holding his head in his hands.

(sl)

"Are you all right? Is something wrong, sir?" Still he didn't move. "What is wrong with you?" they asked, a little louder. Again he kept silent. "Tell us. Tell us what's wrong."

The answer seemed to come from the other side of the bench: "Me. I'm what's wrong." They all turned toward the voice. Squinting their eyes, they made out the outline of a transparent woman. They could see right through her. She repeated, "I'm what's wrong." She twisted around, looking down on her transparent body. Then she ran off, the man stumbling after her.

Late in the afternoon, a transparent woman was swimming in the community pool. She was not aware of her transparency until she got out of the water, grabbed a towel, and began drying herself. She was so shocked, she ran away.

Within a few days, more people turned transparent. It was difficult to keep track of these people. One might see one of them fleetingly and then lose track. The town became alarmed. Clearly, some powerful and mysterious force was at work. The mayor saw to his duty. He called an open meeting in the town hall. It was very well-attended. Indeed, there had never been such a crowd at a town meeting. They formed little groups and chattered about what might be causing the mysterious transparencies.

The mayor, His Excellency, Mr. Roland Eisle, became impatient and pounded his gavel on the rostrum. "This meeting will now come to order. PLEASE. QUIET!" Gradually, the noise abated and attention turned to His Excellency. "My fellow citizens, ladies and gentlemen, as you are aware, our noble little town faces a serious crisis, the likes of which we have never before experienced. It is, to put it simply, without precedent. We need to take counsel among ourselves and determine our path forward. We need to start with FACTS. I want no conspiracy theories. To that end, we shall start with the record, as assembled by our valued secretary, Mr. Sidney Brandt. Mr. Brandt will read the known facts into the record."

Mr. Brandt stood and went to the rostrum with his notes. He cleared his throat and began to recite the facts: "On or about 3:30, the afternoon of the third of September, we had our first report of a transparency. People were startled to see a man run by, fully transparent. We have been able to ascertain that the runner was Mr. Archibald Neally, but we have not yet had the chance to interview him. Another sighting occurred at 4:05 in the city park. A completely transparent woman ran off, with a clothed man stumbling after her. The woman was Rosalind Howell, last seen running toward her house, and her friend was Mr. James Oswald. It is not known if Mr. Oswald went into the house with her. The group that witnessed Miss Howell's transparency also saw a transparent runner pass by. He was later identified as Mr. Richard Welles. Just before 8:00, a lifeguard at the communal swimming pool saw, with difficulty, a fully transparent woman swimming. She started to dry herself, but then turned and ran. We now know that that person was Rachel Teague. There may be others. We know of a fifth transparent person, but that person has yet to be found or identified." With that, Mr. Brandt looked up, bobbed his head and returned to his seat.

Throughout the report, Mr. Eisle smiled with approval. This fact-based presentation pleased him very much. He returned to the rostrum to offer a few observations of his own. "Whatever it is that renders people, men and women, transparent, would seem to also render clothing transparent. These transparent people, I might add, seem to be startled, causing them to run."

"We don't know very much, do we?" said someone in the hall.

"Seems to me that we ought to have a plan," said someone else.

A third piped up: "You got a plan, Mr. Mayor?"

A woman's voice was heard next, saying, "I do hope you have a plan, because it's awkward, being transparent."

Mr. Eisle scanned the room. "Who said that?"

"It was I," came the answer. Mr. Eisle kept searching. "Fifth row, aisle seat. I am the fifth transparent person Mr. Brandt referred to."

At last, Mr. Eisle's eyes lit on the person. "Is that you, Miss Hanley?"

"Yes. And to show you how awkward this is, someone tried to sit on me. Somehow, someone or something has to stop this happening to anyone else."

Mr. Eisle smiled, saying, "Why is it you are not running like all the other transparent people?"

"I came here to hear what you propose to do about this disaster. If you have a plan, I hope it will also reverse all the existing transparencies."

Actually, His Excellency, the Mayor, did have a plan. It might be called, "Pass the buck on up." He drew himself up and read this proclamation: "In view of the complexity and uncertainty attending on the rash of persons assuming transparency in our noble little town of Muellenberg, we urgently appeal to the provincial government in our capital city of Lassinhall, to assemble a commission of experts to investigate the origin of the mysterious transparencies occurring in our noble little town."

There was a general murmur of approval. Miss Hanley, however, stood and ran out of the hall. Mr. Eisle banged his gavel and declared the meeting adjourned.

In the ensuing days, the Provincial Governor, His Even More Imperial Excellency, Mr. Jerome Stallings, worked to satisfy the urgent request in Mr. Eisle's Proclamation. Of course, there were more transparencies reported in that same interval. The task of appointing a commission was difficult, because no one knew what they were dealing with. The result was a motley crew of "experts." Among them were two medical doctors, one of them specializing in virology, the other in neurology, an astrophysicist, a paranormal investigator, a climatologist, a sociologist and, as chairman, a businessman. The businessman was appointed in view of the deleterious economic effects the transparencies might have on the whole province. The others were selected on the assumption that one or another of their fields of inquiry would reveal the force creating transparencies. They met to create the ground rules of their investigation. Again, that was imprecise due to the lack of any firm notion of what they were investigating.

They boarded the train to Muellenberg, took up residence in the local hotel, and met with the Town Council and the Mayor. Then they went off in all directions, some using sensitive machines measuring or tracing energy. Energy, they reasoned, must be behind such upheaval. Others conducted interviews. Naturally, there was particular interest in knowing exactly what the transparent people experienced when they became transparent. They surely would provide some important clues as to how this spate of transparencies got started. With a little luck, they also might lead to how the transparencies could be reversed. Unfortunately, they never could get one of them to stop running long enough to be interviewed.

After much searching the source of the transparency epidemic was revealed. On the edge of the "noble little town" of Muellenberg stood a one-story white building with many large windows. This was the home of the Institute for the Development of Diagnostic Devices, or IDDD. Townspeople knew little about what went on in that building. Moreover, the researchers in the building knew little of the town, as most of them commuted from other towns. Dr. Ejner Ulrichsen, Director of the Institute, was shocked to discover that one of their experimental devices had gone out of control. The device, designed to replace bulky X-Ray machines, consisted of a floating "eye" that could peer inside a body focused exactly on a specific area with the use of a monitor box. One day, the monitor box fell unnoticed on the floor, liberating eyes to float out through the windows and into the town. There, they were given to rendering whole bodies transparent. Without the monitor box, the eyes could not be focused or turned off.

Dr. Ulrichsen reported this to His Excellency, Mayor Eisle, and offered to take care of the problem. This was great news. The mayor was delighted and urged him to do so. It was not difficult to turn off the eyes using the restored monitor box. People were full of wonder as they watched their solid flesh return. It was much more difficult to round up all the eyes, but eventually, even that was done.

At that moment, the whole town erupted in jubilation. There was much singing and dancing in the streets. It was pure joy and ever after the town celebrated "Transparency Free Day."

(sl)

Body Exchanges

A man wearing a grey frock coat and a bowler hat stood with a cane in front of a bank building. He watched two men engaged in an intense argument. One was a tall man who berated the other for some egregious error. Meanwhile, the other, short and plump, cowered under the blast of the accusations. Eventually, the first man ran out of words. He simply glared. After a few moments, he found eleven more words: "You made your bed, now you have to sleep in it." The other man nodded, said he was sorry and walked away.

The man in grey approached the angry man. "Excuse me. I could not fail to notice your impatience with the gentleman."

"Yeah, the guy's a complete jerk."

"I don't suppose there are many incomplete jerks."

"Who the hell are you? This is none of your business. Buzz off."

"I'm sorry. The name's Merwyn. You might not believe it, but that really is my name. I know a few things about you both. For starters, I know his name is Henry Oakes and yours is Franklin Stroud. I also know that you ushered him out of your bank when he wanted to renegotiate the terms of his loan."

Franklin was startled. He studied the man in grey. Finally, he drew himself up in a dignified stance and demanded, "How in the world would you know that?"

"I have my ways."

"Then you probably also know that this fellow Oakes has gotten himself into deep trouble. He wanted to borrow more money on an existing loan and tried to put up a worthless property as collateral. He thought he could get away with it. I wasn't about to let him do that. I've got his number."

The man in grey smiled. "Have you never been in trouble?"

Franklin blinked. "Well, nothing like that."

Merwyn lightly touched his cane to the man's forehead, saying, "Tomorrow, when you have slept in the bed you made, think of this old adage: Do not judge a man until you have walked a mile in his shoes." Saying that, he abruptly disappeared.

Franklin Stroud looked around in some amazement. Then he shrugged and went back into his bank.

Meanwhile, Henry Oakes had been sitting on a bench in the town park feeling sorry for himself. He sensed someone standing in front of him. He looked up. The man in grey had caught up with him and asked if he could share the bench. Henry nodded and they sat together for a while.

Henry then asked, "Did I see you by the bank a short time ago?"

"Yes."

"It's embarrassing."

"Don't be embarrassed, Henry. I happen to know your situation. In fact, I know it in detail."

Henry Oakes was astonished that the man knew not only his name but also his difficulties. He looked at the man and said, "Pretty pathetic, isn't it? I'll never get through this."

"Oh, I think you will. You know, it's a curious thing about money and happiness. Did you ever notice? You can earn money but you can't create it. It's the opposite with happiness. You can't earn happiness, but you can create it."

"Well, maybe I could counterfeit money and be happy."

"Not what I was thinking." Merwyn stood up. He touched the man's forehead with his cane. "Now, I want you to know one thing. Tomorrow, when you awaken, you'll find yourself transformed. You'll be prompted to do something. It will be good."

"How do you know that?" asked Henry.

"I have my ways." Saying that, the man disappeared.

(sl)

The next morning, two strange things happened. Each man woke up in the other man's body. Franklin sensed he had become pudgy and his new belly had caused a button to pop off his pajamas. Henry got out of bed and realized his pajamas were hanging loosely down to the floor. Each went to look at himself in a mirror and saw that he still had his original face. They assumed that meant they had the same heads. The next moment they both sensed this prompt -- they were each to go and find the other.

After some difficulty finding clothes that might make them look less ridiculous, they set out. Franklin had Henry's address from the bank records and Henry knew to go to the bank. They met halfway. At that point, they sensed another prompt. They were to greet one another.

"Good morning, Mr. Oakes. I believe you have my body."

"I do, Mr. Stroud. And you, mine."

"Let me apologize for my rudeness yesterday. You did not deserve that."

"No need, Mr. Stroud. I understand. You were right. I have been careless. You had every right to put me straight."

"I would like to make amends. Allow me to put you in touch with an excellent financial advisor whom I know. Your situation is not so bad that the gentleman can't pull you out of it. He does wonders resolving debt problems."

"I would be much obliged."

"Now, how do you suppose we can exchange bodies?"

"I have no idea how it was done and certainly no idea how it can be undone."

At that moment, Merwyn appeared and declared, "I have my ways." He smiled. He went on to say, "Gentlemen, you have spoken the words I needed to hear." He tapped them on their foreheads and instantly, the bodies returned to their rightful owners. Merwyn was gone.

Of course, there remained one problem. The rightful owners did not have their rightful clothing. They hurried home to change clothes. Over the next few days, Henry Oakes met with the financial advisor who arranged a plan of debt consolidation. It also came about that Mr. Stroud and Mr. Oakes developed a cordial friendship.

Disappearances

Late one afternoon, the people of the bustling town of East Chester began to notice something strange. At that time of day, they had the habit to go strolling through the town park, greeting each other as they passed by. It had always been a pleasant ritual and, no doubt, it contributed to a feeling of solidarity or camaraderie. It was not that everyone knew everyone else, except as nodding acquaintances, but they enjoyed feeling a bond with their neighbors. Now, however, these people had the vague sense that some of their fellow citizens were missing.

At first, it was a matter of simple inquiries, such as, "I haven't seen Pat Pearson in a while," and someone would respond, "I think she must have gone out of town." Then someone else volunteered, "I saw her last Thursday and she didn't say anything about going away." Or people remarked on the absence of Mr. and Mrs. Dauenhauer, and it was suggested they had to attend to some family business. After a while, when no good answers could be had, and Ms. Pearson never

(cl)

did come back from wherever she had gone, the townspeople became alarmed, even more so when the Dauenhauers and others did not return. People were disappearing! All kinds of conspiracy theories floated about town. Some thought the government was eliminating these people, or a secret society was abducting people and enslaving them. A few were convinced that a supernatural power was causing the mass disappearances.

Before this crisis descended on East Chester, Ralph Tidrick fell in love with Melanie Riddell, and she with him. They had grown up in the same town and it never occurred to either one that they would find romance together, yet they did. They spent as much time together as they could, walking in the park, going to the movies, watching sports events, attending concerts, and going out for dinner. As the crisis gradually took hold, they began to hold onto each other. They feared that if one let go, the other would disappear.

Mr. Giannetti, who had a grocery store below Ralph's apartment, laughed at their worry. He was very fond of those two young people, and he told them they were holding on to each other for a different reason. After a week, he himself became concerned and then alarmed, as he realized two of his customers had disappeared, one right after the other. He counseled the young lovers to maintain a distance from one another.

This was an unprecedented phenomenon. It was inevitable that the scientific community would take an interest in what was happening in East Chester. An investigative panel was appointed, consisting of climatologists, microbiologists, environmentalists, poison experts, medical professionals, and even sociologists. They came with all their equipment and testing devices and began to scour the town. Their arrival caused more alarm than relief. Indeed, after they appeared, the rate of disappearances accelerated. Ralph and Melanie held on to each other tighter. The scientists determined that the major contributor to the crisis was an invisible gas that had settled on the town. They had no idea how to pull the gas out of the air. All they could say with some authority was that the gas tended to settle around the warmth of human bodies. Until they could find a remedy, they advised the remaining townspeople to maintain distance from each other. Mr. Giannetti repeated his warning. Movie theaters closed their doors. Sporting events were canceled, as were concerts. Restaurants shuttered for lack of clients or employees. Fewer neighbors met fewer neighbors strolling in the park.

Ralph and Melanie were hard-pressed to maintain any distance from each other. They simply had to be touching. Mr. Giannetti told them their behavior was putting them in danger. But they continued to hold on as they always had.

One day it happened. Ralph lost hold of Melanie. When he realized it and turned to regain his hold, she had disappeared. He stood there in the middle of the street with his arms outstretched, calling out her name. Of course, it was useless. She was gone. He sank to the ground, unaware of the traffic around him. Ralph was inconsolable. He wept and screamed. People tried to help, but he pushed them away. Someone ran to Giannetti's Grocery and told him that Melanie had disappeared and that Ralph was writhing on the street in grief. Mr. Giannetti closed his shop and ran to Ralph, who let him lift him up and take him by the elbow back to his apartment.

There, he calmed down enough to let Mr. Giannetti settle him in his easy chair. Checking the pantry, Mr. Giannetti saw it was nearly empty, so he promised to bring him some food. That was easy enough as Giannetti's Grocery was on the ground floor directly below Ralph's fourth floor apartment. Mr. Giannetti left and returned at once with a basket of food. Between Ralph's sobs, he showed him how he could get more food: the basket had a rope tied to it, a rope long enough to reach the ground floor. All Ralph had to do when he got hungry was to write a list, put it in the basket, call Mr. Giannetti and lower the basket to him.

Through tears, Ralph declared, "I will never be hungry."

"We'll see," said Mr. Giannetti, as he left to return to his shop.

Left alone, Ralph returned to his grief. He grieved, day after

day. He became weak and
quiet. Mr. Giannetti was
quite right: there is nothing
like hunger to counteract an
insistent grief. That was when
he remembered the basket. He
wrote a list and put it in the
basket.

He called Mr. Giannetti,
who came out of his shop and
looked up. Ralph asked him
to fill the basket with the items
on the list. Mr. Giannetti did
so, tugged the rope and called
Ralph to pull the basket up.
That evening Ralph created
a fine little meal. After that,
for the first time in a long
while, he slept well. The
next morning, he returned
to grieving. So began a cycle:
basket/meal/sleep/grieve.

As he followed this
day-to-day cycle, something
interesting began to take place

(sl)

in the town square. A crew brought a huge tanker truck into the town. This machine was designed to spread a particular gas to counteract the toxic gas causing the disappearances. Attached to the front of the tank was a tall snout and at the back, an engine. In preparation for this operation, a car equipped with a loud speaker on its roof circulated through the town, urging everyone to shelter in place.

Ralph, of course, was already sheltering, but he could not help but watch as the engine started up. After a few moments, a pinkish cloud emerged from the snout and began spreading all over town. Finally, in the late afternoon, the engine stopped. People slowly came out of their houses. They noticed that the air had a pleasant scent and hoped it meant the old cloud had been driven away. They whispered among themselves that perhaps now the disappearances would stop. Ralph threw open his window and took in a deep breath.

The disappearances did stop, but not all at once. There were three more in the following days. On one of those days, Mr. Giannetti stepped out of his shop and was startled to see the rope lying on the ground. He looked up. Ralph's window was open, but he was not there. Knocking on his door got no answer. A few townspeople forced open the door and found the place empty. Ralph Tidrick had disappeared.

Now it was Mr. Giannetti's time to grieve. In the midst of his grieving, he harbored a hope that Ralph's disappearance meant his reunion with Melanie. Perhaps, he thought, all those people who disappeared actually reappear somewhere else. It may even be that they have gone to a better place.

A Spark of Life

One afternoon, Alfred Morris died. It was not a surprise. In fact, he was expecting it. He had been planning on it for some time. His doctor calculated that he had six months to live. He muttered to himself that all doctors use that stock phrase. Still, he felt certain his time on this earth was limited. As time passed, he grew more and more curious about what he might find on the other side. After all, no one had ever come back with a report. As a sort of preparation, Alfred read *The Divine Comedy*, but of course, Dante hadn't really come back; actually, he never went. He also read the story of Orpheus, but that is mere myth. Somewhat closer to reality are the reports of near-death experiences, whereby a person felt himself rise up to look down on his body laid out on a bed. Again, those are really not accounts of the Afterlife. Quite simply, no one has come back to tell us.

Alfred decided to rise to the challenge, and be the first to do so. Naturally, that would require careful preparation. Not knowing exactly what to expect made that difficult. He told himself that an educated due diligence would lead him to the right decisions about how to prepare his mind. After all, that is where the soul resides. He felt certain that he should also make every effort to take the tools and devices most helpful in paving his way back.

As to the latter, he was well aware of the old saying: "You can't take it with you," but he told himself that adage applied to money and treasured items -- signs of avarice. He could not be accused of that. He was only thinking of utilitarian things. He would take only such items he calculated might be of use.

To prepare the mind, he called upon a pharmacist whom he happened to know, a certain Dr. Mattingly Musett. This was not the first time that the man had had an unusual request from Alfred Morris. (Perhaps the less said about that, the better.) At any rate, he was accustomed to indulging Mr. Morris' requests, frequently with the use of placebos. This time he filled prescriptions with pink pills to enhance his powers of observation, blue capsules to keep him alert, and red tablets to fend off sleep. All three were placebos.

Alfred turned his attention to useful items to take along. He knew very well that it would be foolish to take anything heavy, such as a stepladder or a shovel. He settled on three items: a camera to photograph the other world, a flashlight to illuminate any dark places, and a pocket voice recorder to record sounds the Afterlife.

He then went to work creating his deathbed. He wanted a comfortable pillow, but there was no need of a blanket, as he expected to rise out of the bed. There was, however, a need for a pocket to hold

(*sl*)

the three useful items, so that they would be easily accessible. He had an uncanny sense that his time had come. He swallowed each of the three pills, thinking this may be his last chance to do so.

Once satisfied with all his preparations, he called his regular physician and laid down on his deathbed. The doctor arrived with a nurse and stood by the bed. Alfred welcomed them both and crossed his arms over his chest. Suddenly, he felt himself rise up toward the ceiling. From there, he looked down on the bed and saw the doctor use his thumb and forefinger to close Alfred's eyes. Then he watched the nurse pull a sheet over the whole body, saying "May his soul rest in peace." As soon as she said those words, Alfred passed through the ceiling.

Alfred now found himself in a shadowy realm where souls were marching toward a distant light. He could only make out their silhouettes. He reached for his camera, but of course, that was in a pocket of the bed where his body lay. Alarmed, he tried to find the voice recorder, then the flashlight. All those things were with his body. Worse, he did not have a body – at least not in the familiar sense of a body. In its place was what he would call a shade, its shape somewhat like the original body. Its darkness set it apart from the surrounding grey world. He saw a distant light. He joined the other shades in a march toward that light. There was nothing else to do.

Alfred was deeply disappointed. Not only was he left without his camera and his recorder, he clearly had no way to return to inform others about the Afterlife. As he emerged into the light, he seemed to lose his shade. What remained was a sort of punctuation mark, to life, an asterisk.

And that was his end; nothing more to be said. Or perhaps not: what seemed an asterisk might have been something with an animating power, a spark of life. That spark might kindle another life, as it may have done many, many times before it brought Alfred to life.

(sl)